My Grandmother's Hands

Written and Illustrated
by
Antoinette Czamara

ISBN: 978-1-7363789-0-8

Published by
Heritage Publishing US
www.heritagepublishingus.com

My Grandmother's Hands

is dedicated to the memory
of my dear friend
Sue.

She was a mother, a teacher,
and the perfect grandmother
to Devan, Eli, and Evan

My grandmother's hands

hold a lasting story

of unconditional love

and her pride in my glory.

A bit wrinkled, but still

nimble and quick,

they've tied up my shoes

And helped when I am sick.

They've hidden a smile

from a joke

that I make.

They've cooked up a meal

and

baked up a cake.

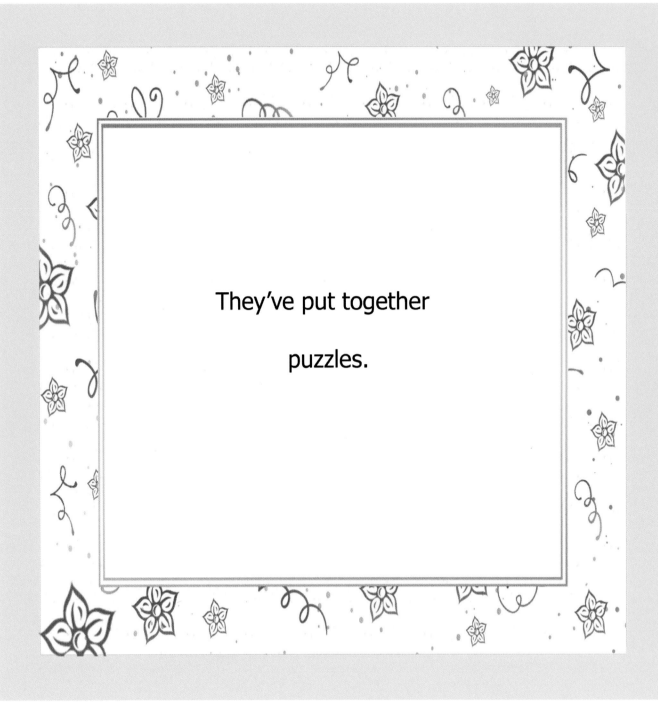

They've put together

puzzles.

And picked up my clothes.

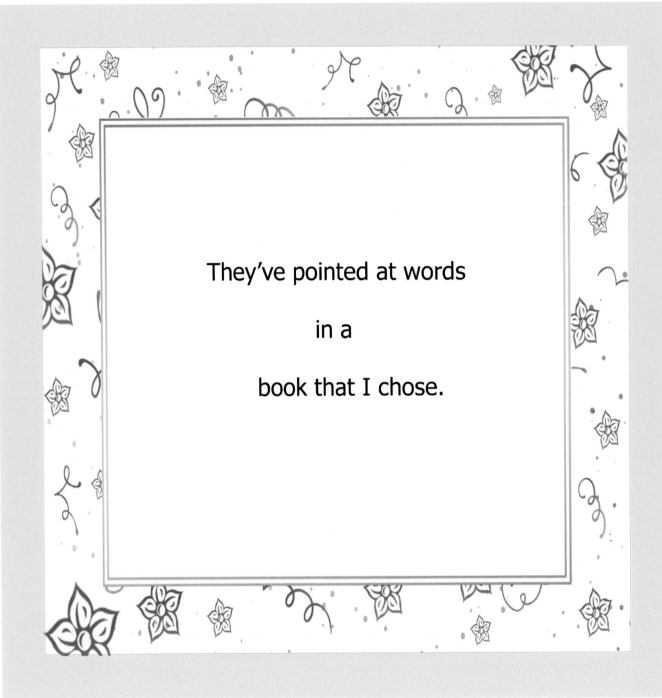

They've pointed at words

in a

book that I chose.

They've stitched up a

costume

for Halloween night

And fashioned a quilt

so warm

and

so bright.

They've clapped at my games

and helped me try harder.

They taught me to write

and

made me grow smarter.

And when Grandma was living

I think that she knew

her hands crafted dreams

for me to make true.

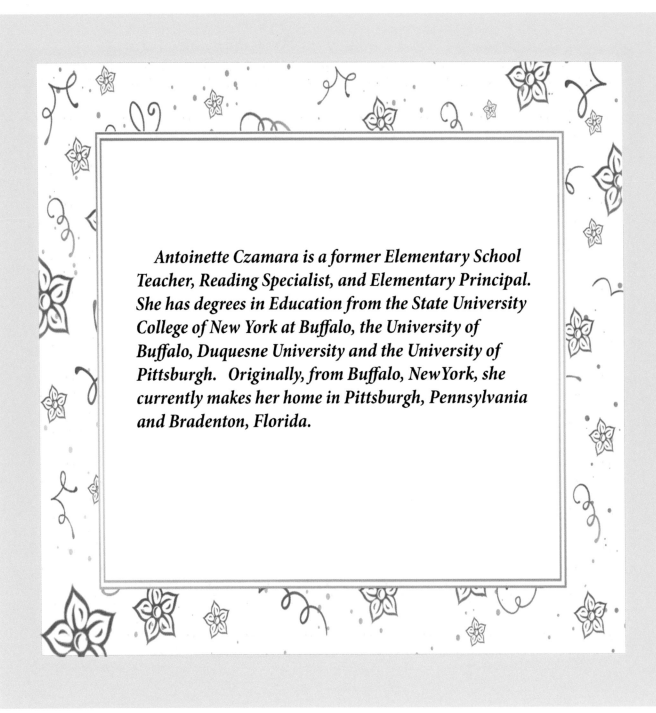

Antoinette Czamara is a former Elementary School Teacher, Reading Specialist, and Elementary Principal. She has degrees in Education from the State University College of New York at Buffalo, the University of Buffalo, Duquesne University and the University of Pittsburgh. Originally, from Buffalo, New York, she currently makes her home in Pittsburgh, Pennsylvania and Bradenton, Florida.

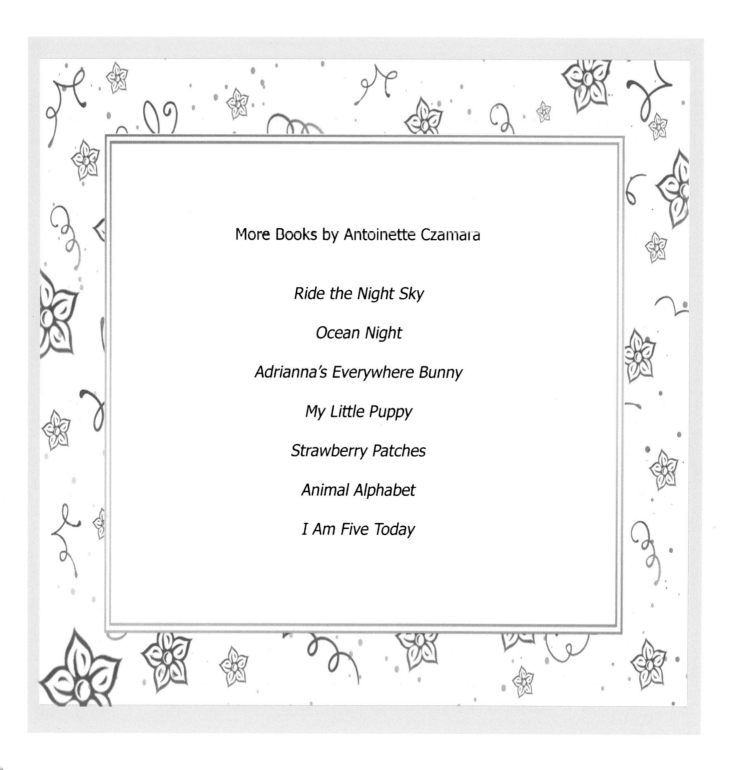

More Books by Antoinette Czamara

Ride the Night Sky

Ocean Night

Adrianna's Everywhere Bunny

My Little Puppy

Strawberry Patches

Animal Alphabet

I Am Five Today

Made in the USA
Middletown, DE
11 October 2024